PAUL

by Karla Kuskin
paintings by Milton Avery
HarperCollinsPublishers

Paul Text copyright © 1994 by Karla Kuskin.   Illustrations copyright © 1994 by the Milton Avery Trust.   Printed in the U.S.A. All rights reserved.   Kuskin, Karla.   Paul / by Karla Kuskin ; pictures by Milton Avery.   p.   cm. Summary: When his parents are too busy to listen to his song, a young boy sets out, with the aid of a fantastic assortment of characters, to find his magic grandmother.   ISBN 0-06-023568-3. — ISBN 0-06-023573-X (lib. bdg.)   [1. Grandmothers—Fiction.   2. Magic—Fiction.]   I. Avery, Milton, 1885–1965, ill.   II. Title.   PZ7.K965Pau 1994 [E]—dc20 93-29424 CIP AC Typography by Al Cetta 1 2 3 4 5 6 7 8 9 10 ❖ First Edition

For March and Sally,
then and now.
—K. K.

Back in the 1940's a writer named Hoffman Hays wrote a children's story that he hoped could be a picture book. Hays's friend, the painter Mark Rothko, suggested that *his* friend Milton Avery might illustrate the story, so Hoffman Hays came to visit us. He liked Milton's work so much that he bought a picture Milton had painted of our daughter, titled *March with a Fishbowl*. Milton was very happy about that and decided to paint some pictures to go with Hays's story. There was a flying pig in the story, and Milton did a sketch of it and a trial painting. He redid his first painting and did seven more gouaches on big sheets of watercolor paper. A publisher accepted the manuscript and pictures, kept them for a long time, but finally decided that the book would be too expensive to print. So Hays took back his story, which eventually was lost, and Milton kept his illustrations. Time went by and another friend who had seen Milton's gouaches said *he* would like to write a story to go with them. More time passed, our friend wrote and wrote, but none of us were happy with the result, including him. We did not want to hurt his feelings so we put away the pictures then and did not try to find another writer. About a year ago this old friend died and March and I decided to ask Karla if she would try to write the story to go with Milton's pictures. We have known Karla since she and March met in school. They were eight years old. Karla had always been a great admirer of Milton's work and was very pleased to be a part of our project. Here are the pictures and story. It has taken quite a long time, nearly fifty years, to get them together.

—Sally Avery

Paul is about your size. He wears shorts all summer and a hat that never blows off. The hat may be magic. It was a present from Paul's magic grandmother. Paul likes to put it on and walk around making up stories, poems, things like that. Monday he put the hat on and started to make up a song.

What do I do when the day is too gray
when the day is too boring and long
when everyone's busy
and no one can play?
I put on my hat
and I hum to myself
I put on my hat
and I talk to myself
or I make up an interesting song.

Paul wanted to sing this to his father but he was busy painting. He said, "I'd love to listen, my boy, but not right now. I'm painting this picture, and I need to get the blue right. Maybe a little later." Paul called his mother at her office so he could sing her his song. Her answering machine said she was busy and could not come to the phone right now. It said she would be happy to call back a little later.

Paul thought about his magic grandmother. He wished he could sing his new song to her. She always loved the things he made up. But she was busy traveling out West so he sat down and wrote, *Dear Grandma, I want to come and sing you my song. How do I get there? Please have supper ready. Love, P.* He was not a really good writer yet but by the fourth copy the letter looked OK. He put it in an envelope, and found a stamp. But he did not know the address so he tucked the letter in his pocket and went outside feeling a little sad.

Paul sat in the warm sun imagining this and that. He imagined that he saw a pig with wings in the pale distance. As it got closer the pig said, "Paul, why do you look a little sad?" Paul explained that everyone at home was too busy to listen to his song but he knew his magic grandmother would love it. He showed the pig his letter.

"A stamp, but no address," said the pig, who looked like he might have an idea. "Do you want your letter to go airmail?" he asked.

"I guess so," said Paul.

"Then climb on my back," said the pig. "I'm flying out West this afternoon. Maybe you can find your grandmother and give her your letter yourself."

"Great," said Paul, but he wondered if he really could find her. "Isn't the West very big?" he asked, and the pig said, "Very, but there's no harm in trying . . . or flying." He tucked Paul's letter under one wing. And they zoomed into the blue.

They flew along for some time and the pig said, "Did I remember to tell you that I am forgetful?" This worried Paul.

They flew some more and the pig said, "Did you say you wanted to mail a letter?" This worried Paul more. He wondered if the pig remembered that they were flying out West to find his magic grandmother.

They flew even more. The pig said, "Did you say she is magic?" Paul nodded. "How?" asked the pig.

"Well," Paul shouted over the wind, "my father says her cooking is magic (especially supper), this hat she gave me is probably magic, and my mother says her friends are magic."

The pig thought for a minute. "Oh," he said. "THAT magic grandmother. I think she is a friend of mine."

Paul reached out and touched the air speeding by. It was cool and damp. Below him he saw little mountains, a winding river, and tiny trees. The Western train chuffed over its track, looking as small as a caterpillar. Paul made up a new verse for his song.

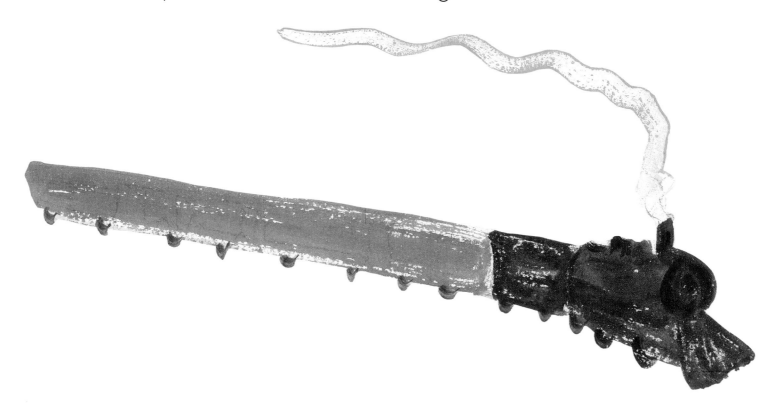

Is the sky dry?
Is the air wet?
Is it far now?
Are we there yet?
If the day is too gray
or the trip is too long
I make the time pass finding words
for my song.
I rustle up words and I whistle a tune
and not too much later
I get there
I get there
I get there
quite soon.

We are here, I think," the pig said. "Here" was a strange place. There was a strange far-off hill with a strange far-off house on it and a strange flower the size of a tree at the pond's edge. The pig had put on fancy wings and a crown.

The trouble began when Paul asked for his letter and the pig said, "A letter? To a grandmother? I had it under my wing?" They looked everywhere but it was gone. The pig must have dropped it somewhere between there and here, or when he changed wings.

"Oh, it will turn up," he said. Then he pointed to a very large blue-eyed caterpillar whose tail was a cloud of smoke. The caterpillar reminded Paul of the Western train. "He used to be a train," the pig explained. "He has been many places and seen many things. Maybe he can help you."

"Excuse me, my dear Caterpillar," Paul said politely, "I am trying to find my magic grandmother. I want to sing her my song. The pig with wings thought you might be able to help me." The caterpillar explained shyly that he could not see very well without his glasses so he had not noticed any magic grandmothers lately. But he did have an idea.

"Make a wish," he whispered. He gave Paul one of his whiskers. "It's a magic wish-ker (little joke)," he whispered. "Wishing doesn't always work, but give it a try." Paul held the wishker tightly and wished for a policeperson who could give him directions.

The sun set looking like a fried egg.

The moon rose looking like a smiling marshmallow. Stars popped out. A big fish floated in the dark blue sky. Paul's legs looked sky color too. He saw the police-person he had wished for standing near three pine trees. The magic wishker grew into a wishing wand. So much was happening so fast that Paul had to add a new verse to his song.

18

I stood with a wand
at the edge of the pond
wishing a wish
that turned into a fish
and rose like a kite in the sky.
I thought thoughtful things
about pigs that have wings
and fish that can fly.
And I wondered, if they can,
can possibly I?

Paul was pleased with his new verse but the sky fish said in an annoyed voice, "Of course you can fly, Paul, can't you see your wings?" Paul peered at his reflection in the pond. A large white gull had just fastened a pair of big wings to the back of his shirt.

"These may help you find your magic grandmother," the gull squawked softly. "You can fly from place to place just like a pig." Paul thanked the gull. He liked the idea of being able to fly. He couldn't even ride a bicycle.

Before he zoomed off Paul spoke to the plump police-person. "Excuse me, Officer," he said politely. "I am trying to find my magic grandmother so I can sing her my song. I wonder if you can direct me." He also explained about his lost letter.

"Should turn up," said the policeperson. She had a short, snappy way of talking. "Very big place out here," she said. "Many magic grandpersons." Paul was afraid he would never find his grandmother when the police-person said, "Hang on, there is one especially nice grandperson who cooks up a delicious supper like magic, gives magic presents, hats and things, talks animal language with her friends, hardly any accent at all."

"That MUST be my grandmother," said Paul, getting excited but trying not to let it show.

"Ever been to the Plains of Pure Pleasance?" the officer asked snappily. Paul shook his head. "Very far place," said the policeperson. "F-A-R. Look for her there. Listen up for directions." Paul listened closely and he made the directions into a verse so he would remember them. He added the verse to his song.

Over the ice and over the snows
I must ask the North wind where to go
as he blows.
If I hold my wand in my strong left arm
and draw a red circle to keep myself warm
I will make the next step
and will come to no harm.

Suddenly the North wind rushed in blowing snow before him in every direction. Even the smallest trees were taken by surprise and the birds were breathless from being blown backwards. Paul was brave. He took the policeperson's advice and stood in the red circle. He did not get cold and, of course, his hat did not blow off. Then Paul had a conversation with the wind. "Excuse me, Mr. North," he said very politely. "The policeperson thought you might be able to direct me. I am trying to find my magic grandmother so I can sing her my new song." He also explained about the lost letter.

The wind, which had been blustering fiercely, stopped for a minute and hummed softly. That meant he was thinking. Then he spoke and his voice sounded like a low howl blowing through a thousand trees. "The letter will shooowww up." He howled, "Howwww is she maaaagic?"

"Well," said Paul, "her cooking is magic (supper especially), her presents are magic (for instance, my hat), and her friends are magic."

"Oh, THAT magic grandmother," the wind said. "She is really faaaaar. To begin with you must ask the singgggging cat." Paul listened closely to the wind's directions and made them into a verse so he would remember them. He added the verse to his song.

I must go over the ice and over the snows
not skinning my knees
not freezing my toes
and then wander under the sweet apple trees
(they follow the ice and the snows
and the freeze).
I will not lose my way
or my heart
or my hat
until I lay eyes on the great singing cat.

"One lasssssssst thing," whistled the wind. "You may need a shovel for the applesssss." When the wind said those words, Paul's wand became a shovel, and he wished himself over the night, into the day, and out from under the sweet apple trees.

Milton Avery '46

The singing cat was practicing long tones. "Meeee meee mee," she sang, almost on key. Then she sang, "Ooow wow wow." It was not beautiful but it certainly was loud. She might never have stopped except Paul said, "Excuse me, Ms. Cat, I am looking for my magic grandmother. The North wind said you might be able to help me."

"MEEOWW," sang the cat very loud one last time. Then she looked right at Paul. "Do you like to sing?" she asked. Paul was going to tell her about his song when she noticed the shovel. "Ah," she said. "Clever of you to bring one. We would have needed it if you hadn't brought it, but because you did, we don't. Apple season just ended twenty minutes ago."

Paul looked so disappointed that she hurried to explain. "In apple season it absolutely rains apples. You have to shovel yourself out of here. Applesauce all over the grass, pies in the skies, and in really hot weather the trees are full of baked apples. Don't be disappointed," she said. "You can thank your lucky stars it's over." She pawed through her songbook, and Paul was afraid she might start singing again and never give him directions, but she looked at him with eyes as big as green apples and said, "You must be the one who lost the letter." He said he was. "It will turn up," she meowed. "Hmmm, that means you're the one looking for a magic grandmother."

"Yes I am," Paul said politely.

"How is she magic?" the cat asked.

Paul explained about the magic cooking (especially supper), and the magic presents (he showed her his hat), and the magic friends, and the cat said, "Oh, THAT magic grandmother. She is a friend of mine," just the way everybody else had. She was really very helpful. Paul listened closely to her directions, made them into a verse, and added them to his song.

It just may be snowing and blowing
it may not be easy or nice
I must watch for the prowlers and growlers
who live near the Mountains of Ice.
The valley is wide and the valley is slick
I will need a strong wish and a spell-casting stick.
The valley is slick and the valley is wide
and I have to get to the opposite side.

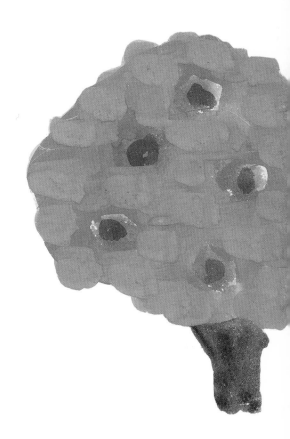

Of course the cat must have been magic too because as soon as she meowed those words, Paul's shovel turned into a spell-casting stick and then and there he wished himself to the foot of the White Ice Mountains. It was so cold that he used another wish for a fuzzy pair of slipper socks. Then, holding the green stick tight, he looked around at the wolves. No question about it, all four of them were very large prowlers and growlers. But Paul spoke to them in his politest tone and never looked directly into their eyes because that only upsets a wolf. "Excuse me, dear Wolves," he began. "I'm looking for my magic grandmother and the singing cat thought you might be able to help."

Two of the wolves went right on prowling, the third kept on growling; but the fourth rolled over, wagged his tail, and said, "Certainly, dear lad, in what way may we help you?"

Paul explained that he had to get across the White Ice Mountains to the Plains of Pure Pleasance to find his magic grandmother.

"Is she the magic cooker?" asked the first wolf.

"Supper especially," said Paul.

"And does she give magic presents?" asked the second wolf.

"Like this hat," said Paul.

"And does she have magic friends?" asked the third and fourth wolves.

"Everywhere," Paul answered.

"Oh, THAT magic grandmother," the four wolves howled together. "She's a friend of ours."

"I thought she might be," said Paul. Then the wolves growled directions to the Plains of Pure Pleasance. Paul listened closely and made them into a verse so he wouldn't forget them. Then he added the verse to his song.

It may not be easy
it may not be nice
I must wish myself over
the Mountains of Ice.
I must pass through the Meadows
of Partridge and Pheasants
where antelope lope
near the Low Hills of Hope
till I come to the Plains of Pure Pleasance.

"And rememberrr," the youngest wolf grrred. "You will know you are there when you see the old deeerrr." Paul thought it was rude to call his grandmother an old dear but he didn't think he should argue with a wolf. So he held his breath and wished his wish and it worked just like the magic it was.

Milton Avery 1946

Grandma

His grandmother was busy with her pots and pans. She called out, "Hi, Honey, I've been expecting you," and made a delicious supper so quickly and easily it seemed to be magic. "How did you know I was coming?" Paul asked, and his grandmother said, "I got your letter." She pointed it out. "Deermail," she said.

That's when Paul saw the old deer. A real one with antlers. They looked something like the wings the sea gull had given him. After supper when the deer fell asleep, Paul's grandmother explained that the wings, the antlers, the wands, and the wishkers were all manufactured by the same magic company. Paul asked about the deer's buttons and she told him that they were for keeping the deer's coat snug in cold weather.

"He used to have a very nice zipper but it got stuck last January, so I put on buttons," she said. Paul told her about his trip including the pig with wings, the blue-eyed caterpillar, the plump policeperson, the North wind, the singing cat, and the four wolves. She looked worried at the places that were worrisome and she laughed at the funny parts. By then Paul was so sleepy he forgot to sing her his song.

The next morning the sun came up over the edge of the green grass. There were little white flowers everywhere. A spring chicken hunted for breakfast worms and three butterflies circled and dove for dew drinks. Paul began to sing. He sang every verse he had made up. He sang until he came to the end of his song.

His grandmother loved it. He knew she would.

THE END

Milton Avery

Most picture books begin with words. An illustrator (who may be the writer and may be not) works with a finished story, bringing it to life, augmenting, commenting, illuminating with the art. Then there are those picture books that start with a visual idea. In such cases the artist would also be the writer, using a picture or series of pictures as a starting point and structure for a story. But working on this book was not like either of those processes. I was presented with all the pictures. They were very detailed, very finished. The only aspect of them I was free to change was their order. I felt a little as if I had been sent on a mystery treasure hunt. The clues included the winged pig, that very large buggy creature, the dark-haired child, fish in the sky, the wolves, etc. . . . How could all these odd creatures, fanciful details, and scenes be connected into a believable tale? Staring long and hard at the pictures, writing and constantly rewriting, I kept trying, not so much to invent a story as to discover the one in Milton's pictures.

—Karla Kuskin